TRAINS, SCOTS AND PRIVATE EYES

CONNOR WHITELEY

No part of this book may be reproduced in any form or by any electronic or mechanical means. Including information storage, and retrieval systems, without written permission from the author except for the use of brief quotations in a book review.

This book is NOT legal, professional, medical, financial or any type of official advice.

Any questions about the book, rights licensing, or to contact the author, please email connorwhiteley@connorwhiteley.net

Copyright © 2023 CONNOR WHITELEY

All rights reserved.

DEDICATION

Thank you to all my readers without you I couldn't do what I love.

CHAPTER 1
Inverness, Scotland
3rd July 2022

Private Eye Bettie English didn't really know what to make of her amazing boyfriend Graham's suggestion about touring Scotland before their twins were born. She loved Scotland, the Scottish people and really supported them (sometimes very few English people actually did), but going there on holiday?

Bettie had always firmly believed that a holiday meant going somewhere abroad, hot and sunny (and ideally filled with hot sexy men on beaches), so she wasn't entirely sure about going to Scotland or anywhere in the UK for that matter.

But as Bettie sat on a wonderfully soft chair with a large metal table in front of her in a little café, Bettie was so pleased that she had come here. The little café was filled with rather interesting Scottish paintings and even from inside she could still hear the gentle roaring of the River Ness.

That was something that had surprised Bettie, considering how massive River Ness was with multiple impressive bridges having to stretch over it, she was expecting it to be loud and noisy and horrible. But she was wrong.

There was something so calming about watching and sitting and talking with Graham near the River Ness.

Bettie returned her attention back to the little café table and picked up the last bit of her shortbread dessert. The entire meal had been amazing and even though Bettie sadly couldn't have animal products because her pregnant body didn't agree with it, the Scots definitely knew how to get creative.

Whatever Graham had ordered the Scots had managed to create a vegan version for Bettie without a single piece of fuss. That never would have happened in England and it only spoke to how kind, helpful and generous the Scots were.

Bettie placed her last piece of delicious shortbread in her mouth, and her mouth exploded into a buttery symphony of flavour. There was so much depth to each bite from the buttery deliciousness that was melting in her mouth to the gourmet sweetness of the vanilla, all the way to the amazing sweet, velvety kick of whatever they used instead of sugar.

It was amazing.

Bettie smiled at her amazing boyfriend Graham

in his wonderfully tight (but stylish) blue jeans, blue shirt and boots that made him look stunningly sexy, and Bettie already wanted to show him that later.

But after spending the past week and a bit scratching the surface of amazing Scotland, Bettie was a little sad that they were leaving. They had explored the breathtakingly rich historic city of Edinburgh, Glasgow and then the Lochs, from Loch Ness to all the others.

That had been so beautiful.

And now Bettie and Graham were spending their last full day in the capital of the Highlands, a breathtaking region of Scotland where there was nothing but rolling hills, nature and the freshest air Bettie had ever experienced.

It was even more surprising that Bettie was still inside and she could smell the freshness of the crispy air. Bettie really didn't want to leave, but she still had some backgrounds to check for clients and there was no doubt some cases that prospective clients wanted her to investigate.

Bettie rested her hands on her baby bump (which was rather big at this point) and she just stared at the stunning love of her life Graham, and simply smiled.

Sometimes she actually forgot how lucky she was, Graham was the most amazing man she had ever met and he was just so beautiful. And thankfully after Bettie helped him with some police corruption cases, there were rumours of Graham getting promoted, which would be great with the babies coming (not that they needed the money, Bettie seriously had enough).

"What did you want to do this afternoon?" Graham said.

Bettie loved his voice.

"I don't know. Walk around. See the sites," Bettie said.

Bettie looked past Graham's shoulder and focused on the very cute little entrance into the café, which was made up of a golden desk, a pot of free Scottish Shortbread and small bottles of Scottish whiskey to buy. But something was off.

A rather young man had walked into the café, looked around and gone out straight away.

Bettie didn't know why it bothered her, it just did.

"Everything okay babe?" Graham asked.

Bettie nodded.

"Good. We could go to the Cathedral," Graham said.

Bettie slowly shook her head. "You know I don't like going to Christian places out of respect for Sean,"

It wasn't like Bettie was really trying to be difficult, but ever since her nephew had come out as gay and revealed all the abuse he had received (hell some religious person had tried to kill him and his boyfriend last month), Bettie just wasn't comfortable providing support to an organisation that unwillingly taught people to hate gays.

It just didn't feel right to Bettie.

Graham smiled and nodded. "I think it's free,"

Bettie smiled. "Okay. We can go,"

Then the young man from earlier came back in, looked around and saw Bettie. Bettie didn't know if that was dangerous or anything, but something still felt so strange about it.

The young man left.

"What's wrong?" Graham asked.

"There's a young man who keeps looking at me. He pops in and out of the café. Like…"

But Bettie didn't know what he was being like, it felt strange.

Then the young man came into the restaurant and walked over to Bettie and Graham.

Bettie looked at Graham and they both frowned. She had a feeling that they weren't going to the cathedral, and something was about to ruin their last day in Scotland.

When the young man got to Bettie, she reckoned he was rather attractive with his short blond hair, broad shoulders and fit body. But he was easily twenty-five years old, why would he be interested in Bettie?

"Miss English?" the man said, clearly Scottish.

"I am," Bettie said, "who are you?"

The young man looked around, saw the coast was clear and he pulled a chair over to sit with Bettie and Graham.

The young man lost his accent. "I am Agent Carter, MI5. Your friend Agent Daniels told me I could trust you,"

Bettie and Graham both smiled at each other. She hadn't thought about Agent Daniels, the Russians or anything from that rather interesting case a few months ago for ages. But clearly MI5 were grateful for Bettie's help and if memory served it correctly (which when it came to money it always did) Her Majesty paid very well.

"Where's Daniels?" Graham asked.

"Top secret," Agent Carter said.

Bettie shook her head. "Mr Carter, you have ten seconds to tell me why you're here before me and my boyfriend leave?"

"He said you were efficient," Carter said. "How would you like to be part of a special tester programme?"

"Testing what?" Bettie said folding her arms.

"The UK Government is transporting a number of people back to London tonight," Carter said, "Including a very important member of the Scottish Government, her Majesty's Government would prefer non-agents to be on the train,"

Now Graham folded his arms. "Because everyone knows how the English always protects Scottish people,"

Bettie smiled. That was something she always liked about the Scottish, they made sure they protected themselves, because it was clear from every bit of research she had done that if the UK Government had to choose between English and

Scottish lives. They would choose English for sure.

Bettie wasn't a fan of that. Scottish and English were still part of the UK, everyone should be protected equally.

"In a way yes," Agent Carter said slowly.

"Payment?" Bettie asked.

"Five thousand pounds for the safe arrival of all occupants," Carter said, passing Bettie an envelope. "Details are in there, see you at 9 pm,"

As Bettie watched Carter walk away, she couldn't help but feel like something was very wrong.

No one just hired a cop and a Private Eye for the fun of it.

Something larger had to be going on.

And that concerned Bettie more than she wanted to admit.

CHAPTER 2
Inverness, Scotland
3rd July 2022

Graham had seriously enjoyed the past week and a bit with his amazing girlfriend Bettie. It had really been the most fun he had had for years, they were both constantly talking, laughing and joking.

It had been wonderful.

Even the little café now was a rather interesting blend of poshness with the coziness of the Scottish Highlands, and Graham was still surprised at the freshness of everything.

The wonderful smell of the piney fresh air with hints of smoked salmon, buttery shortbread and herbs filled the entire café, and it was such a powerful but amazing smell that Graham flat out loved.

Graham might not have been too hopeful about Scotland before he came here (he had only suggested it as a joke) but now he was here, he was amazed. Every single expectation he had had was wrong.

Before he left England, all his cop friends had been (not) joking with him about watching out the hateful crazy Scots that hate the English. But after the past week and a bit, Graham had to say that the Scots were some of the nicest, kindest and most generous people in the UK.

And they can seriously cook!

Graham was definitely going to have to cook some of those Scottish dishes again. Graham really loved a dish he just had with crispy, succulent fish and golden potatoes that were just hard enough to have a satisfying crack, but not too hard to break his knife. It was the best fish dish he had had in ages.

But Graham wasn't sure about Agent Carter.

In all his experience as a cop who had worked with different branches, department and sectors within law enforcement, Graham knew better than to just automatically trust everyone.

There were so many political battles in law enforcement alone, that more often than not, if someone wanted you to do something, it was probably just because they wanted to use you to their own ends.

And that was why Graham had slightly forcedly suggested to Bettie they go on holiday before the babies come. He had said it was because he wanted to remember their loneliness and just be a couple with kids one last time.

But it was because he just needed to get away from the police. After everything that racist, homophobic and stupid senior officers had put him through recently. He just had to get away from them all.

Graham smiled at Bettie as she kept watching the entrance of the café as probably in case Agent Carter came back.

Since the Agent had left five, ten minutes ago, Graham had made a few phone calls to his friends at Kent Police (in England), his friends at MI5 and he had thankfully managed to get a very short phone call with his friend Skylar Mason, who was the UK's Justice Secretary.

They all said the same thing.

There was no official record of a train leaving Inverness tonight and arriving in London ten hours later.

Now Graham wasn't too surprised there, because whilst Kent Police did occasionally get called into London to help with their security if there was a big event. They didn't always.

And it wasn't like his friends at MI5 would always tell him things, and there was a good chance this train was off the records on purpose.

But it really bugged Graham that Skylar Mason didn't know a thing about it. From all the conversations she had had with Graham and Bettie, she always sounded like she knew exactly what the government was doing, including the more secretive affairs.

She didn't have a clue on this occasion.

Graham quickly told Bettie everything he had found out, and then Bettie unpacked everything in the envelope and neither one of them were too impressed.

All the envelope contained was a single sheet of paper detailing where they needed to be and what they needed to bring at 9 pm, and they shouldn't tell anyone.

Graham had already broken that rule.

"Does something feel wrong to you?" Bettie asked.

Graham laughed. "Of course babe. MI5 doesn't just tell us to do something. There's a reason for this,"

Bettie leant closer. "They said they're transporting a member of the Scottish Government,"

Graham nodded. He had no idea why that was important.

"And I don't understand why they would need to transport one of them secretly down to London. It made no sense. The Scottish Government has its own security and bulletproof vehicles,"

Graham nodded that was a good point. It really made no sense.

"What if," Graham asked, "this is a secret-secret meeting? A meeting that neither government wants their own people to know about?"

Bettie shrugged. "That would be the most likely option. We've seen all the posters this week, there is a massive mood for independence,"

Graham laughed. Bettie shot him a look. It was no secret that Graham didn't like the idea of Scottish Independence, but he was starting to change his mind on that, especially now he knew that the Scots weren't just troublemakers.

Graham stood up and took out his phone. "I think we might need some help here,"

Bettie smiled and waved her own phone at him.

"What?" Graham asked.

Bettie laughed. "Remember. I bought that black market Phone Encrypter the other week, if MI5 are making sure we don't tell any people about this, best I make the secret calls,"

Graham nodded, he did love how Bettie bought all the latest (very illegal) gadgets that she only ever used for good.

Graham knew exactly who she was talking to, she would only be talking to her wonderful nephew Sean who Graham really liked too. He had been watching the office whilst Graham and Bettie were away, and he should still be there now so hopefully Sean could go to sleep now and be on call if they needed anything.

Graham just hoped that Sean was okay looking after his boyfriend Harry by himself. Graham still felt awful about leaving them both because after Sean and Harry were attacked last month, Harry had suffered brain damage. Making it hard for him to have balance, remember certain things and say certain words.

Thankfully he was responding well to therapy,

but it still didn't make Graham fill any less guilty about leaving.

"Bye Sean love you," Bettie said.

Graham looked at her. He really hoped she had some good news.

"Turns out Harry prefers the nighttime anyway. He's in bed at the moment," Bettie said, "so Sean said he'll hop in with him, sleep through the day and be at the office for us tonight,"

"Brilliant!" Graham shouted.

It wasn't until now Graham realised how excited he was about tonight.

A secret train journey sounded seriously fun!

And Graham couldn't wait to find out why they had been called in.

CHAPTER 3
3rd July 2022
Inverness, Scotland

Standing on the extremely long train platform that curved to the right, Bettie stood in the biting cold nightly air and even though it was only 9 o'clock at night, it was pitch black.

Bettie had partly expected there to be a bit of light on the horizon, but this far north that was never going to happen, at least it added a bit of atmosphere.

Bettie didn't know why but she couldn't help but feel like the pitch darkness only made her want to focus on the strangeness and secret nature of the entire operation. Normally, Bettie and Graham would have stood in the warmth or inside the actual station itself.

Yet if this wasn't what it seemed then Bettie wanted to be able to see someone coming as soon as possible, and put this mystery person and herself as far apart as possible. She didn't know why she was being so paranoid, she just was.

Bettie loved the amazing refreshing smell of the country highland that made the air smell so fresh, crisp and cold, leaving the wonderful taste of freshly cut grass on her tongue. It was amazing.

Graham stood next to Bettie in his very attractive trench coat, hiking boots and thick trousers that made him look like some Private Eye from the 30s or something. And Bettie was rather surprised he managed to pull it off.

After they had left the café, Bettie and Graham made sure to use their time wisely, they had both had a few hours sleep to make sure they wouldn't be tired on the train journey. And they both had had a great Scottish dinner, and Bettie had even got to a little known spy shop in Inverness to get a few things.

Truth be told, Bettie still wasn't sure what she had actually bought. She had simply picked up three items, thrown them in a bag because a cop walked in and paid for them.

After that Bettie had been too scared to open it in public, so that spy bag was safely tucked away in her suitcase that her baby bump was resting on. Graham had laughed at the sight, but it made Bettie feel better.

The eerie silence on the platform was broken when seven people walked onto the platform from different directions, and it was far too dark for Bettie to see them clearly, but there were definitely seven people.

Bettie wasn't sure if these were all friendly but judging by how slowly and carefully they were walking, they were clearly as concerned about them and the other people as Bettie was about them.

Clearly no one was fully in the know about this train journey which only made this all stranger. Bettie had been expecting some sort of person in charge who would greet them, sort them out and serve their every whim on the train.

That wasn't happening. Sadly.

And after everything Bettie had heard from other Private Eyes, experienced herself and been taught from Graham, if something felt wrong. Then something normally was seriously wrong.

Bettie just didn't know what yet.

Then Bettie noticed that six of the people walking the platform had stopped tens of metres away from her and Graham, but one person was walking towards them.

After a few moments, Bettie started to notice it was a young man, maybe 26, wearing a large black coat, smart trousers and carrying two large rucksacks that made a banging sort of sound.

"You for the train?" he said.

Bettie might not have been a fan of his brown beard, constant staring at her boobs and his awful smile, but he sounded nice enough.

Graham wrapped his hand round Bettie's.

"We are," Graham said. "Who are you?"

The young man smiled. "I am Leon Zinc, server

and Train Master for this journey,"

Bettie didn't know what to make of him. He seemed nice and normal enough, but there was something just felt off about him. He didn't look like he would be in charge of a train, passengers and making sure everything ran smoothly.

"You're driving the train?" Bettie asked.

Leon laughed. "No Miss English. I would never do that. This train is being controlled by the fine folks in London. There is no driver, such the UK's latest computer programmes all controlled by good English people in London,"

Bettie frowned. That didn't make her feel better.

Leon stepped closer. "And between you and me, I'm glad the Scots aren't controlling it,"

Bettie decided to play his game. "Oh but why?"

Graham laughed quietly.

"Because Miss English," Leon said, "they would probably try to kill us,"

With each passing second Bettie was really starting to understand why she had been called here, but she still wasn't sure *who* had actually requested her presence.

The sound of buzzing, humming and vibrating filled the air as a rectangular train eased it's away into the platform, and considering this was meant to have the latest computer programmes on it, Bettie couldn't say she was too impressed.

"That's the grand computer programmes!" a woman shouted.

Bettie smiled as she saw all six people walk over to her, Graham and Leon as the train stopped in front of them.

Now the train had stopped, Bettie noted how it was only a single carriage with two large windows with a table in front of each and a driver's compartment was at the front.

It still didn't fill Bettie with too much confidence to say the least.

Bettie nodded to each of the six people as she looked at them and their luggage. There were another three men in addition to Leon, and three other women. Bettie couldn't see them too clearly but she was sure once they were all on the train, Bettie could have a chance to get to know them, and investigate why they were there.

"This cannot be the train," a woman said.

Now they were all so close, Bettie saw it was a very short little elderly woman who was clearly English wearing a little coat, a black dress and some massive high heels. Even if Bettie wasn't pregnant she doubted she could wear them.

"Miss Mia Ford," Leon said, "as the government explained, we are testing this. This is a prototype for something far, far grander,"

Bettie still couldn't figure out who these different people were. She would have to have a good talk with each of them later, because there was one question she couldn't figure out.

Why bring together seven people (not including

herself and Graham) who didn't know each other?

Especially if it was only for a test run of some new train.

Something wasn't right.

And that concerned Bettie more than she wanted to admit.

CHAPTER 4
Inverness, Scotland
3rd July 2022

Graham had always been a massive fan of travelling by train, there was just something so amazing about it that you always missed by travelling by plane or car.

It was probably because on an actual train you could simply relax, lay back and simply watch the breath-taking world pass by without you having to do anything.

So as Graham and Bettie sat on some very comfortable train seats at the very back of the carriage, Graham was really looking forward to the journey.

Or at least he was going to try.

Considering this was meant to be a very modern train controlled by computers and people in London, Graham had imagined there to be something scifi about it. But there was none of that.

The entire train carriage was a simple enough design with two plastic tables in the centre of the carriage with two seats each side of the walkway going back 4 rows.

Not exactly fancy so that definitely was a letdown, but Graham was rather interested in why go to all this length and use a normal everyday train carrier. There had to be a good reason, especially considering this was probably as off the books as you could get.

Something was strange about this entire thing. And Graham had to find out what.

But as much as Graham loved train travel and he wanted to relax, Graham and Bettie did actually have to do something, and Graham couldn't decide if he liked any of this so far.

As he saw it he had been thrown onto a small train carriage with seven strangers and his stunning girlfriend, without being told why they were hired and who everyone was on the train.

Sooner or later Graham just knew he was going to have to talk to everyone and try to give them to spill details of their lives to him. And as amazing fun as that was, Graham just wanted to absorb the atmosphere for a little bit.

The entire train carriage smelt of sweat with hints of pine, shortbread and cherries filling the air, and that the absolutely amazing taste of cherry shortbread form on his tongue. Graham loved that taste!

Yet everyone in the train carriage was completely

silent. Graham and Bettie were sitting in the far back near where everyone's suitcases were, two men and two women were sat around the tables in the middle and then Leon Zinc was in the driver's compartment doing something.

Leaving the very last person to board the train who was a middle-aged woman who choose to sit at very end on the opposite end of the train.

Normally Graham wouldn't have suspected that person to be dodgy, scary or some kind of criminal. Yet out of everything Graham had seen of this woman, he doubted she was a danger.

Granted Graham didn't really have a chance to look at her properly so far. Maybe she was hiding something, definitely someone he needed to talk to.

"Excuse me everyone!" Leon shouted as he came out of the Driver's compartment at the opposite end of the carriage.

Everyone looked at Leon, who was now wearing a very weird looking outfit that could only be described as looking like a Bell Boy.

"Thank you all for coming. I am your Server for this journey and I am Train Master. My name is Leon Zinc, and I'm afraid I have to go over some critical rules,"

Graham just looked at Bettie. Neither one of them were impressed.

"This is a top-secret train journey. And if you look at your phones you will see there is no service. You cannot use Wi-Fi, mobile data or phone service during this ten hour ride to London,"

Graham really didn't feel good about this.

"Also the train is controlled by computers and the good folks in London have direct access to the systems. But I must warn you, this train cannot be hacked, and once we start moving it will not stop,"

Graham stood up. "Not even in case of emergency,"

Leon laughed. "Of course not. This train will not stop for any reason, and we have basic medical supplies and plenty of food just in case,"

That seriously didn't make Graham feel any better.

"We will set off in a few moments then dinner will be served at mid-night. We will arrive at London at 7 pm tomorrow morning," Leon said.

Graham watched him turn away and go back into the Driver's compartment.

"This isn't good," Graham said. "How are we meant to talk to Sean and Harry?"

Bettie shook her head. "I might have bought something earlier to help us. But this is serious Graham. I'm never heard of anything like this, we need to talk to these people and answer the question,"

Graham cocked his head. "What question?"

Bettie smiled. "Why the hell bring all these people together on a top-secret train journey?"

Graham jerked forward as the train started moving and the air was filled with the sound of humming, banging and vibrating.

Now they were moving Graham's stomach tensed.

It had begun.

Graham and Bettie were now trapped.

Whatever happened in the next ten hours. They were alone.

Completely.

CHAPTER 5
3rd July 2022
Somewhere In Scotland
09:58 Hours Left

Bettie really hadn't been sure on the whole train travel idea at first, it wasn't that she was against it. She had actually rather enjoyed travelling up to Scotland by train and seeing all the brilliant English and Scottish countryside go past them.

It was definitely picture worthy.

But when Bettie was told she would be on a top-secret train, she just managed to surprise herself because she was both excited and scared of the experience. She had watched far too many action, adventure thrillers lately where evil criminals took over the train. But that wasn't going to happen here.

She wouldn't let it.

And the smell and taste of cherry shortbread on her tongue was definitely worth this job alone. She had never smelt something so amazing, and even after a few moments, she didn't really hear the constant humming, banging and vibrating as the train zoomed along the rails.

But Bettie still couldn't understand why other people weren't talking to each other. It was so strange that no one seemed to know each other, and the other woman was hiding alone at the far end of the train carriage was a little odd.

Bettie managed to see her a lot better than Graham had apparently managed, so Bettie saw she was a middle-aged woman wearing a long black dress that made her look very stylish, elegant and powerful.

But as a woman, Bettie knew the look. It was a look of a woman who was heading somewhere who didn't feel safe, secure or like she had any allies. So she needed to look powerful to try and stop people from preying on her.

Bettie hated it how a woman even needed to dress like that, and even though she was with Graham and didn't really go out too often without him. Bettie always tried to look as imposing (and friendly at the same time) just in case.

She had made the mistake of looking like an innocent, weak pregnant lady before. Never again!

"Watch the others," Bettie said, "I want to see their reaction when I talk to each of them,"

Graham nodded. "O, talk to that Mia Ford first. She looked like she knew Leon,"

Bettie kissed him quickly then she slowly stood up and watched as all eyes looked at her. She didn't feel comfortable in the slightest.

Bettie went over to the two plastic tables where three men (Graham must have missed one) and two women were sitting, and they all stared at her.

From what Bettie could understand, the three men were basically wearing the same black business suit, black shoes and they all had different watches on their wrists. Bettie wasn't a massive fan of them because she was absolutely terrified of them being some sort of government agents.

Bettie had to be careful.

But now that Mia Ford had taken off her coat, Bettie really liked the little black dress she was wearing and her golden necklace, rings and earrings made her look very rich and powerful given how short she was.

The other woman sitting near Mia simply raised the newspaper she was reading and covered her face. That was just rude and unneeded.

Mia gestured Bettie to take a seat.

"So you're the famous Bettie English," Mia said, clearly impressed.

Bettie knew she had a reputation all over the UK and her cases frequently went in the mainstream news and even the ancient things called Newspapers, but Bettie was still always amazed when people recognised her in public.

"And that's your cop boyfriend Graham Adams," Mia said.

Bettie nodded. "Yes, but I'm much more

interested in who all of you are?"

Mia smiled like all (in Bettie's experience) posh idiots do when they think they're so much better than everyone else.

"I am Mia Ford, Heiress to the Ford Empire,"

"Wow. The car brand," Bettie said.

Everyone laughed.

"No," Mia said, bitterly. "Of the Ford Luxury Hotel and International Travel Empire,"

Bettie looked at the men. "And you people are?"

The men smiled and looked away.

Bettie leant closer to Mia. "Do any of you know each other?"

Mia frowned. "Nope. I have never seen a single person on this train before,"

"And that is how it was designed," Leon said as he exited his compartment.

"Why?" Bettie asked.

"Miss English. I don't know why. I don't know any of you. I was simply told be here tonight. Check your names against the Guest List and help out,"

Bettie gave him a half-smile. "Who's your boss?"

Leon shook his head. "Above your pay grade,"

Graham walked over and placed his hand on Bettie's shoulder.

"Actually," Bettie said, "judging by the awful Bell Boy costume, the secretive nature of the train and… the expensive smell of your aftershave. MI5,"

Leon frowned. "You cannot know that,"

Everyone laughed.

"Seriously," Bettie said, "your name isn't even real. Come on, Leon Zinc. What? Did your parents like metal and didn't like you as a child?"

Leon really frowned. "Actually that is my name!"

Leon spun around and stomped back into his compartment. Bettie blushed. She almost felt sorry for him.

"Tell me Miss Bettie," the oldest of the three men said. "Do you like Scotland?"

Bettie noticed the woman at the back of the carriage focus on her.

"Of course. It's a great country with a lot of potential if the English would give it enough rope,"

"Hopefully enough rope to hang itself," the man said.

Bettie wanted to gasp or something. That was an outrageous comment.

"Who are you?" Bettie asked firmly.

"My name is Alexander Bell,"

Graham stepped forward. "Property Developer or something,"

Alexander's face turned red. "Or something? Mr Adams I run a billion pound development company, all the work I have done for the Government has transformed lives, revitalize communities and stopped poverty. I am a hero to the UK,"

Bettie noticed the woman hiding was silently laughing to herself.

"Then why do you want Scotland to hang itself?" Bettie asked.

Alexander length closer. "Because the UK Government wants to siege a bunch of land and I have the exclusive rights to build on it,"

Graham shook his head. "The UK Government can't do that unless… you're going to blackmail the Scottish Government to allow you to do that,"

Alexander shrugged. "It's Politics. It's Business. It's Life,"

Bettie shook her head as she recognised the political slogan of some more far-right elements without the UK Government.

Now Bettie was really starting to understand why she was invited on the train. She had only spoken to two people and it was clear something strange was going on.

A Property Developer and an Heiress. It made no sense.

But Bettie wanted to find a connection.

There had to be one.

And it had to have something to do with the woman hiding at the back.

Bettie had to talk to her.

CHAPTER 6
3rd July 2022
Somewhere, Scotland
9:30 Hours Left

Graham was not impressed by the ambush by one of the men in black suits who was clearly getting on with Alexander Bell perfectly.

All Graham had done was simply nodded to Bettie when she said she wanted to talk to the woman who was hiding at near the driver's compartment, but clearly that wasn't what Alexander Bell and his friend wanted.

But if the situation wasn't strange enough to Graham, it seemed like Leon was pretending to polish the door to the Driver's compartment and he occasionally looked at Graham and Bettie. That was weird to say the least.

For the past ten minutes that felt like hours this random man had been lecturing Graham and Bettie on principles of public health, and so much rubbish that Graham was flat out suspicious.

And if he wasn't a cop by day, he wouldn't have put anything past it, he probably would have imagined this man was just another posh snobby person who loved being the centre of attention.

But he was a cop by day.

And clearly these men did not want Graham and Bettie talking to this woman, that was strange to say the least.

But Graham had to admit Bettie did look really cute as she stood there pretending to hang onto every word this man said.

"And by the way, I am Doctor Noah Duncan, Public Health Expert at the… well, that's sorta classified," the man said.

Bettie bowed slightly and Graham firmly shook his head. But Graham just found this even stranger, so now they had an heiress, a property developer and a public health expert on a secret train. And as much as Graham wanted there to be a link, he couldn't see one.

Of course if he could contact Sean and Harry back at the office, it probably would have been a lot easier, but that wasn't going to happen unless Graham could find out a way to unblock phone service.

Graham really doubted he had the skills to do that, he didn't even know how someone would do that in the first place.

Graham looked at Noah. "It's been great talking

but we have to go,"

Graham gently grabbed Bettie and pushed forward so they could get closer to the woman no one wanted them talking to.

Leon shot back into the Driver's Compartment.

"Leon doesn't look pleased we're coming," Graham said.

Bettie nodded.

The hiding woman weakly smiled at them as they came closer, but Graham could see the fear, horror and probably some relief that they were coming in her eyes. Whoever this woman was she was scared of something, and as much as Graham didn't want to think about it, it had to be someone on this train.

"Graham Adams," Graham said as he extended his hand.

Leon appeared as the Driver's compartment door opened and he rolled in a metal trolley filled with large takeaway containers that appeared to be piping hot.

"Everyone! Please return to your seats. We're about to eat," Leon said.

Graham and Bettie both stood firm.

"You said we weren't eating for another few hours," Graham said.

"Why is it whenever we want to talk to this woman, someone stops us!" Bettie asked, loudly.

Graham looked around and everyone on the train was weakly smiling. He couldn't help but feel like everyone knew the reason but they didn't want to share it.

Leon frowned. "Sit down!"

Graham and Bettie looked at each other, and Bettie smiled. Graham recognised that amazing sexy smile and it meant that she already had enough information, and Graham understood why.

Everyone on the train might have tried (badly) to hide the fact that they knew each other, but they did. Graham just couldn't figure out how yet.

But he and Bettie would.

Graham and Bettie slowly went back to their seats on the very back of the train near the suitcases, and they made sure to look at everyone as they went past.

To Graham's surprise, when they reached the middle, the woman sitting with Mia and covered her face with a newspaper was still doing so.

There was a lot more than one person hiding themselves here. But Graham couldn't understand why.

Graham went in first then Bettie sat down next to him, and they dropped down the plastic tables that were built into the backs of the seats in front of them.

A few moments later, Leon gave them each a takeaway container of some sort of curry with their name. Graham opened it and the most amazing smell of coconut, chicken and Indian spices filled the air. It smelt amazing.

Bettie was about to eat it when Graham gently placed a hand on hers, then he took the container and poked around it with a terrible plastic fork Leon gave them.

"Just checking if it's okay," Graham said quietly.

The last thing he was ever going to do was allow Leon, some underpaid government chef or someone else to mess with Bettie's food, or give her something bad.

But after cutting open some of the vegan chicken, tasting it and stirring it around, Graham released a breath he didn't he was holding when he knew it was perfectly alright.

Bettie kissed him briefly. "Thanks anyway,"

Graham nodded. He was always going to protect her.

Something hit the floor.

Something splattered.

Someone choked.

Graham and Bettie shot up.

The Hiding woman was choking.

No one helped her.

She was choking to death.

CHAPTER 7
3rd July 2022
Somewhere, Scotland
9:29 Hours Left

Bettie was just shocked that no one was helping.

She stepped in the Hiding Woman's curry on the floor as she gathered her.

It was even stranger that the woman actually wasn't choking, she couldn't breathe whatsoever.

The woman clucked at her throat. Then Bettie realised that she had to be having some kind of allergic reaction to the curry.

The woman strained herself. She seriously couldn't breathe. Time was running out.

Bettie's eyes widened. "We need an EpiPen!"

No one helped.

Graham looked around.

Bettie shook the woman. They had to find hers.

Bettie pointed to the luggage.

Graham ran down the train. He started to search

the luggage. No one was helping him.

Everyone just sat there watching.

"Leon!" Bettie shouted.

He slowly walked over to Bettie and smiled at her.

"Get me the medical supplies!" Bettie shouted.

Leon shook his head.

Bettie jumped up.

Throwing him against the wall.

"I might be pregnant. But get me a fucking EpiPen now!"

He nodded.

The woman fell to the ground.

Leon bought out the medical supplies.

Bettie grabbed it. Searching through the kit.

She found a pen. Her hands were shaking.

Leon knelt down next to Bettie. He stabbed it into the woman.

He collapsed.

He was choking.

The pen was poisoned.

Both of them were struggling to breathe.

Mia Ford ran over.

Waving an EpiPen.

Bettie took it.

Stabbing it into the Hiding woman.

And Bettie laughed as the woman who had been so damn hard to talk to finally started to breathe on her own, and thankfully Bettie's twins kicked inside her in happiness. Bettie was damn well proud of herself.

Then she noticed that Leon Zinc was no longer breathing and he was just lying there with his eyes closed like he was sleeping peacefully.

He was dead.

The Hiding Woman slowly forced herself up and sat back in her seat, and Bettie was surprised at how strong she looked considering what had just happened.

Then Bettie dipped a finger into the woman's curry (trying to forget it had been on the floor) and Bettie almost gagged at the overwhelming taste of peanuts.

Bettie just looked at the woman. "Someone really wants you dead,"

The woman laughed. "Welcome to my world Miss English. That's why I hired you,"

Bettie's mouth dropped.

Bettie knew she had been curious to find out why and who had ordered MI5 to hire Bettie and Graham for the trip, but she was still surprised that the woman would so clearly admit it.

"As soon as you're done for preliminary bits, we need to talk," the woman said.

Bettie smiled. This woman sounded so calm, safe and secure despite her almost dying less than a minute ago.

"What if you die before we can talk?" Bettie asked.

The woman smiled again. "Miss English, I'll tell

you three things. You're damn well good at your job, everyone on this train wants me dead and nothing is as it seems. Wake me up in two hours,"

Bettie laughed as the woman nodded her head almost like a *Good Night* gesture, and she simply went to sleep. She didn't really know whether to be shocked or not. Whoever this woman was, she was clearly no stranger to near-death experiences.

Bettie laughed a little and then turned around. She just wanted to punch everyone on this train for not helping a woman in danger. Bettie was pregnant and she still helped her. It was outrageous these (rich, wealthy) idiots hadn't even lifted a finger.

But Mia Ford had. And the more Bettie focused on her the stranger it seemed, considering Mia was now rapidly tapping her foot on the floor. Like she was a nervous wreck about something.

Graham carefully stepped over the body and subtly handed Bettie a small black bag that she had bought from the spy shop earlier in the day. Bettie nodded her thanks and really hoped there would be something useful here.

"Start taking pictures, survey for any forensic evidence and make sure no one touches the body," Bettie said.

"Stop!" Alexander Bell shouted. "Who the hell made you in charge?"

Bettie and Graham both laughed.

"I'm sorry Mr Bell," Bettie said coldly, "but I am in charge no matter what. I am a Private Eye who actually helps people and I would like to remind you Graham is an officer of the law,"

Noah smiled. "Yea in Kent. That's the opposite side of the UK at the moment. He has no jurisdiction,"

"Wow," Bettie said, "only the rich would say something like that. Only the rich would be worried about jurisdiction when there's been a murder and an attempted murder,"

Everyone on the train shook their heads.

"This ain't murder," the third man said.

Bettie had no idea what his name was, but she felt like she was about to find out. One way or another.

"And you would know that because?" Bettie asked.

"I am Detective Inspector William Jones of The Metropolitan Police,"

Bettie rolled her eyes. The last thing she needed was a senior detective from London on the train.

"And if this case falls into anyone's jurisdiction it is mine. London is closer than Kent and I was personally contacted by MI5 to their-"

Bettie waved him silent. "I don't care who you are in London. On this train I am in charge,"

That shut everyone up and Bettie loved that feeling.

"Graham," Bettie said.

Graham nodded, and Bettie knew that he would keep everyone in line and he would start to investigate.

And Bettie wasn't too worried about someone organising a mutiny against her. At the end of the day the train would stop in less than ten hours and then everyone would flee and go into the wind.

Bettie went into the Driver's Compartment and shut the sliding door behind her.

Then she realised she had less than nine and a half hours to find out who the killer was and protect the attempted murder victim.

If not, she would never find the killer.

And Bettie refused to have that on her conscience.

She just didn't know if she had the skills to pull it off.

CHAPTER 8
3rd July 2022
Somewhere, Southern Scotland
9 Hours left

Graham seriously wasn't impressed with all the silly guests on this train. They absolutely had to be some of the most awful, stupid and condescending idiots he had ever met. And Graham had met some proper idiots in this time as a cop.

And as for that stupid Detective Inspector, Graham hated him with a passion. It was completely out of order of him to constantly be checking what procedures, methods and techniques Graham was using.

Graham so badly wanted to tell him to go and do one. Graham was rather amazed his patience had lasted this long.

"Want some evidence bags?" DI William asked.

Graham shook his head because he knew for a fact that William was only taunting him, he didn't have evidence bags.

And thankfully Bettie had popped out of the Driver's Compartment a few minutes ago and bought Graham some plastic food bags. It was far from ideal, but considering it was meant to be impossible to stop the train, get help and organise a real crime scene unit to examine the scene. This was the best Graham could do.

He knelt on the cold floor as the train hummed, popped and vibrated as it raced along the rails.

Graham had just about managed to spoon some of the curry that contained too many peanuts into a plastic bag, then he had tied it up.

Graham looked at the corpse of Leon Zinc who was still looking like he was sleeping peacefully and would wake up at any moment. Alexander Bell and the other men had tried to move the body but Graham firmly ordered (and threatened) them not to.

It seemed like there was nothing wrong with the body whatsoever. There were no wounds or any signs of outward trauma, but Graham still got photos of the body, where everyone was sitting and the area around the body. Just in case he needed it.

Then Graham looked at Leon's right hand where he was weakly holding the EpiPen with his thumb still holding the end of the pen. It was clear that Leon knew how to stab an EpiPen into someone in distress.

But why didn't he help sooner?

Graham slowly touched the pen and took it away

from Leon and popped it in a bag. That's when he noticed a needle had come out of the top and it was covered in Leon's blood. Then Graham checked the bottom of the EpiPen where the real needle was meant to be, the needle used to give the drug to the allergy sufferer, and save their life.

There was no needle.

Graham frowned to himself as he realised that this pen was meant to kill the user, and make sure the person on board never got the lifesaving drug they needed. This was unthinkable but Graham had to admit, it was clever.

It was one thing to poison someone with a peanut allergy with personalised food. It was quite another to go to extreme lengths to stop that person from getting the drug they needed, and it was extreme to try and kill anyone who was inclined to help them.

Was that why no one wanted to help?

Did everyone know about this?

Graham took a few more photos of the body, the pen and the injection site on Leon's body.

"Who knew about the poisoned pen?" Graham asked.

Mia Ford continued to just look down at the floor, but everyone else simply smiled. Except for the woman who kept hiding her face with a newspaper.

"You all knew, didn't you?" Graham asked.

"Detective Adams," William said, "I don't know how you Southerners conduct your investigation but in London-"

Graham just glared at him. "We are not in London. We are not anywhere where you have power. We are on a top-secret train. With a killer on board,"

William laughed. "There is no killer onboard,"

Graham smiled. "What do you know? Convince me this isn't a murder,"

"If this was a murder," William said, "then MI5 never would have allowed it. We were all heavily vetted before we came here. The only people we don't know are you two,"

Graham laughed. "So you do all know each other?"

William frowned, folded his arms and turned away from Graham.

Graham was relieved to finally have it confirmed that everyone here knew exactly who each other was, but there were still so many questions that had to be answered.

Graham looked at the Hiding Woman who was thankfully breathing in a deep sleep and she was ever so quietly snorting to herself. Graham didn't know who she was, but he was definitely going to ask her.

Now Graham knew that there was a solid connection, as soon as Bettie came out of the Driver's Compartment, and hopefully (seriously hoping) who was calling for help, they were going to have to start interviewing people.

Then someone would certainly crack and reveal how everyone was connected.

But as Graham stared at the woman sleeping

peacefully, he had no idea why anyone would want to kill her.

When she had been talking to Bettie, she seemed so kind, calm and respectful. She was probably the only person like that on the entire train, so why kill the only good person on the train.

Unless the answer was simple.

What if Graham and Bettie had walked into a viper's nest?

A group of vipers ready to kill.

But the question was why?

Why do any of this?

CHAPTER 9
3rd July 2022
Somewhere, Southern Scotland
8:45 Hours Left

Bettie was not impressed in the slightest. This was flat out ridiculous.

As Bettie sat on a very uncomfortable metal seat in the middle of the circular driver's compartment, there were all types of switches, computer screens and buttons all around her on a control panel that curved around the edges of the compartment.

It was just ridiculous.

If this really was such a high-tech piece of kit, then Bettie had no idea why the hell they needed so many switches and buttons. Bettie had tried most of them for the past forty-five minutes or however long she had been in here since the murder.

And Bettie was hardly impressed by the disgusting smell of sweat, curry and spices that had stunk out the entire compartment. Bettie hated the smell even more because she could smell hints of chicken, beef and duck, which her oversensitive pregnant body was not a fan of.

Bettie forced herself not to focus on the awful smell and she just listened to the constant popping, humming and vibrating of the train as it zoomed towards their destination.

But after pressing a few more buttons, Bettie just shook her head. This was absolutely fruitless and clearly she wasn't going to find a way to contact anyone in London for help.

Even that was a little odd for a government vehicle and Bettie couldn't understand it. What if the train had been attacked by terrorists? What happened if it crashed? What happened if anything went wrong?

And if this really was such a high tech piece of kit, why on earth would the UK Government risk anything happening to it without a way to contact the train just in case?

Something seriously wasn't right here, and Bettie needed to check with her Private Eye contacts had about this secretive train journey, because if Bettie had learnt anything in the past few decades it was how resourceful and clever her fellow Private eyes were.

One of them had to have high-level friends in the government and the security services.

Bettie picked up the small black bag that she had grabbed from the spyware shop earlier in the day and opened it.

Bettie knew she should have checked it earlier but the last thing she wanted was a cop seeing her in a spyware shop. It was one of the first things the owner of the shop had warned her about when Bettie started to ask about the more *real life spyware*, and not the joke stuff the owner sold to the tourists.

Bettie smiled as she pulled out a Satellite phone, a micro-camera (like the one Bettie always used in cases involving affairs) and a mini-flare gun. Bettie had not been expecting that in the slightest, but at least it explained the £200 price tag.

The satellite phone was a large black block of hardware, and Bettie had no doubts this was military grade or something. If anything was to survive a possible train crash, it was probably this phone.

Bettie flipped it open and dialled Sean's number.

"Hello," a young man said who clearly wasn't Sean or Harry.

Then it twigged that Bettie was talking to Agent Carter.

"Where the hell is my nephew?" Bettie asked firmly.

Bettie listened to Carter past the phone over to Sean.

"Auntie," Sean said, clearly annoyed. "This guy with you?"

"What happened?" Bettie asked, trying to contain her rage.

"Me and Harry got into your office at half eight then this idiot forced his way in and threatened to arrest us if we didn't do as he said,"

Bettie sighed. This was why she didn't like working with the security services.

"Put Agent Carter back on," Bettie said.

"Hello," Carter said.

"Don't you ever threaten my family again. And if you hurt them, I swear I will find a way to kill you," Bettie said, firmly.

She had no idea if she would. But she would definitely hunt Carter down if anything happened to her family.

"The Sat phone's a nice touch Miss English," Carter said. "Don't worry your family will be safe unless they endanger National Security by talking about this train with anyone else,"

Bettie bit her lip. "I need them,"

"Because that Scottish bitch is dead," Carter said.

Bettie flat out couldn't believe his arrogance but she understood it. How dare MI5 know about a possible assassination of a Scottish Politician, and they simply did nothing.

It was outrageous.

What made it even more outrageous to Bettie was, she knew for a fact if an English politician had been threatened, MI5 would have been all over this train.

"Actually," Bettie said, smiling, "she's alive. Leon Zinc is dead,"

Carter went silent.

Bettie listened to the phone exchanging hands.

"What do you need Auntie?" Sean asked.

Bettie whispered into the phone. "Sean. If you need it, there is a very old and small pistol taped to the top of the bottom desk draw. Use it if you have to. Protect yourself and Harry no matter what,"

"Okay I can run that check for you," Sean said.

Bettie sighed. She really didn't like the idea of Sean and Harry being alone with Carter, especially with him watching them constantly. She just hoped Carter wouldn't do anything stupid to him.

"And also run the names William Jones, Mia Ford and Leon Zinc for me," Bettie said.

"Got it," Sean said.

The phone changed hands.

"Miss English," Carter said, "I hired you because you were meant to stop all this. You are nothing but a failure. Fix it or your family pays the price,"

The line went dead.

Bettie was furious. She hated Carter, this train and his arrogance towards the Scottish.

Bettie wasn't going to let him hurt her family.

She had to solve this murder.

She had to talk to the Scottish woman.

CHAPTER 10
3rd July 2022
Somewhere, Scottish-English Border
8:41 Hours Left

Graham really didn't like being this far away from the body. He was too concerned that someone might try to damage it, contaminate evidence or gather something he had missed.

Yet he did understand why Bettie wanted to interview the Hiding Woman, also known as a Scottish Politician, away from the rest of the train's guests. One of them was a murderer after all, and clearly she was the centre of everything.

Graham was still shocked from when Bettie had told him about Agent Carter holding Sean and Harry prisoner. He was even more shocked about he was happy to let a UK citizen die.

As Graham and Bettie stood surrounded by luggage on racks at the very back of the train, Graham looked at the Hiding Woman who was clearly excited to see them both. Yet she still kept checking the rest of the guests, probably to make sure no one was charging at her.

Graham really disliked seeing someone like this, he wanted to help them, support them and protect them. He never wanted someone else to be scared.

In case Bettie noticed something he didn't, Graham looked at her briefly and she too wasn't pleased to have this woman clearly scared. They both wanted to help her and protect her.

But Graham had to admit Bettie was so beautiful standing there with her stunningly beautiful face, hair and just how she stood there looked damn well adorable.

Graham seriously loved her.

"Spoke to Carter?" the Hiding Woman asked.

Graham smiled. He was actually rather impressed the woman knew what they had done so far.

"You weren't sleeping were you?" Graham asked.

The woman smiled. "Course not. Good thinking with the plastic food bags for collecting evidence,"

Graham nodded his thanks. Yet he found it so unnerving that this woman was meant to be a Scottish politician but she sounded so English, and she didn't have any trace of a Scottish accent in her voice.

"No accent?" Graham asked.

The woman really smiled. "I am Aubrey Armstrong. I work for the Scottish Government and whilst no one ever sees me publicly too often. I am the second most powerful woman in Scotland after the First Minister,"

Graham nodded. She really was a politician. She hadn't answered his question yet.

Aubrey took a step closer. "Officially, this train is meant to take me to a meeting with your Prime Minister in London. I and him are meant to be discussing Scottish Independence and a new referendum,"

Graham rolled his eyes.

"You aren't a fan?" Aubrey asked.

Graham was about to answer when he realised how kind she sounded. Normally when Graham had bumped heads with a politician in the past, they had yelled, shouted or made him feel like some kind of idiot.

Audrey didn't.

She actually sounded like she wanted to understand where Graham was coming from, and like she wanted to learn from him. He had never experienced a politician being this respectful before in his life.

"Sorry," Graham said, "I just don't see the need. Scotland is part of the UK. You get to vote and you get MPs in the UK Parliament. You have your voice like the rest of us,"

Graham saw Bettie sigh. He knew he was probably completely wrong about Scottish politics, but unlike Bettie he had never found the time to research it all.

Aubrey nodded. "I completely agree. Yet no

offence, Scotland has been ruled by a UK government we haven't voted for since 1955. Ever since Scotland might have voted overwhelmingly for their own government, but we haven't been ruled by a government we wanted for decades. Is that democracy?"

Graham could understand that. He guessed he would be quite annoyed if he lived in a country that voted for something, only to be denied that because a stronger, larger country had voted for something else.

"And that is why I am meeting your Prime Minister," Aubrey said.

Graham was shocked again by this woman. Normally politicians banged on about their causes and beliefs for hours. Not Aubrey. She wanted to crack on with what actually happened given the situation.

"And unofficially?" Bettie asked.

Aubrey again checked the other people on the train.

"This train is meant to kill me," she said.

Graham frowned. "How?"

Aubrey took a few deep breaths. "Our First Minister is unofficially banned from entering England, so she sent me here. Back in Scotland I am one of the critical brains behind the push for Independence,"

Bettie smiled. "You think someone wants you dead to stop the push,"

Aubrey just looked at the other people on the

train.

"There are so many reasons why people want me or what I represent dead. That's why the First Minister contacted her remaining friends at MI5,"

Both Graham and Bettie gasped.

"You probably don't know. But if an official request comes from Scotland, it's normally denied, or dragged back for as long as possible depending on how much the request is in the media. If a request comes from an English MI5 officer, it's normally accepted,"

Bettie stepped closer to Aubrey. "So you got someone in MI5 to get Carter to hire us,"

Aubrey nodded. "Your friend Agent Daniels is a good man. He actually cares about all of the UK,"

Graham stepped closer to them both. "What connects all of you? How does everyone know each other?"

Aubrey's face just dropped. "That's the thing Graham. I don't know. I don't know these people. But they clearly all know each other,"

"And they sure as hell know you," Bettie said.

Aubrey gently grabbed Graham's arm. "And they know about my peanut allergy. Believe me, not even my NHS doctor knows that,"

"It's not on any public medical record then," Graham said to Bettie.

Graham just looked at both the women. "Then who the hell are we dealing with?"

Both women just shrugged.

And that concerned Graham greatly.

These two were clearly intelligent. So was Graham.

And no one knew who could be behind this.

Graham had to find answers.

He had to talk to Mia Ford.

CHAPTER 11
4th July 2022
Somewhere, Northern England
7:00 Hours Left

Bettie had never ever met such annoying idiots in her entire life. Not only had these horrible people witnessed someone die and not tried to help, they knew about poisoned medical supplies and didn't say anything and to top everything off. They did not want to talk to Bettie.

All Bettie had been trying to do for the past hour and a bit was solve the case. She had tried and tried and tried to talk to Alexander Bell, Doctor Noah Duncan and the rest of the idiots.

No one wanted to talk.

And that Detective Inspector had even had the audacity to accuse Bettie of being the killer herself. That was outrageous and now Bettie fully understood why Graham wanted him to be the next murder victim.

Bettie stood with her arms folded as she stared at Mia Ford who was still refusing to talk, but she kept tapping her foot rapidly against the floor.

She was nervous. Bettie just wanted to know why exactly she felt nervous considering everyone else around her was acting so cool.

"You must know something Mia," Bettie said calmly.

Graham walked, locked the Driver's Compartment, and Bettie was relieved Graham had decided that was the safest place for Aubrey to be.

"Talk with us," Graham said to Mia.

Bettie was surprised when Mia actually stood up and followed her and Graham down to the other end of the train with all the luggage.

Bettie blew Graham a kiss. She had always loved the amazing power he had over people, he could be commanding, but he did it in such a way that he just made people feel safe and like it was in their best interest.

For Mia it definitely was.

Mia pushed herself into one of the racks holding all the luggage. Bettie wasn't sure if she was trying to get away from her or trying to remain out of sight of the others.

Probably the latter.

"Tell us everything Mia," Bettie said.

Mia shook her head.

"We won't let them hurt you," Graham said. "You're nervous about something. Why?"

Mia laughed and gestured to the rest of the train.

"You see a dead body before?" Mia asked, stressed. "I never seen one. It scary,"

Bettie wasn't buying it. "What links everyone on this train?"

Mia's face went blank. Bettie couldn't see a single piece of emotion, stress or anything.

"I will not tell you," Mia said.

"Are you allergic to nuts?" graham said.

Bettie smiled. "Not Graham's nuts. Normal nuts. Like peanuts,"

Graham playfully hit her.

Mia frowned. "No,"

"Then why carry a drug for allergy sufferers," Bettie said, turning around and checking the luggage labels.

"Why you looking?" Mia asked.

Bettie smiled. She actually didn't want to find anyone's luggage, she only wanted to see Mia's reaction, but now she had it. Bettie wanted to find hers.

"What links you all?" Graham asked.

"Nothing," Mia said.

Bettie found Alexander's luggage. It was a horribly heavy black suitcase, but she didn't want it. She had to find Mia's.

Bettie looked back at Mia. "If I phone someone, will they confirm you're the real Mia?"

Bettie didn't know why she asked that question, but she realised it was an interesting one to ask.

Mia grinned. "You can't phone anyone,"

Bettie turned back to Mia. "Innocent people don't focus on that detail. Innocent people would say *'of course I'm the real Mia Ford, who else would I be?'*"

Mia frowned. "I am the real Mia Ford, who else would I be?"

Bettie didn't buy it, and judging by the massive smile on Graham's face. He didn't buy it either. So why is Mia Ford lying about who she was?

Was anyone on this train who they said they were?

Was Aubrey who she said she was?

Bettie pulled Mia out the way and started searching the other racks for her luggage.

"Now tell me Mia," Bettie said, "why would you pretend to be an Heiress. They aren't powerful, much liked or even respected,"

"Why be anything on this dammed train?" Mia said, grabbing a small suitcase from the rack.

Graham went to grab her.

She whacked him away.

Mia opened the suitcase.

Whipping out a syringe.

She thrusted it into herself.

She pulled down the plunger.

Graham ripped the syringe out.

But as Bettie rushed forward to help she quickly realised that the damage was done, there might have been half of syringe full of clean liquid left, but Mia slipped away.

As she fell into Graham's arms, Bettie helped him to slowly lower her to the ground, and Graham checked for a pulse.

"She's alive. Just very unconscious," he said.

Bettie carefully looked at everyone else in the train who had slowly moved closer to them. It was just by a seat or two (or three for the really brave), but they had clearly wanted to be closer.

"I think we should check the rest of these bags," Bettie said.

Graham nodded. "Have you seen our bags?"

Bettie looked around quickly and realised that their bags weren't onboard.

"They never put out bags on the train," Bettie said.

Graham pointed to the floor, and Bettie noticed how lines and even a very small hole in the floor.

"They bought our bags on board. They opened up the floor and threw our bags away,"

Bettie cocked her head. "But how did you get me by spyware bag earlier?"

Graham grinned. "I covertly attached it to Alexander's bag. I had a feeling something strange might happen,"

Bettie kissed him. This was why she loved him. He was just amazing.

The Sat Phone started to ring and Bettie was really hoping that Sean and Harry were still alive.

Graham placed a hand gently on her arm. "Remember Mia wasn't who she said she was, so is

Agent Carter really who he says he is?"

Bettie gulped.

She hated that idea. She didn't want her family anywhere near him.

The idea of Carter not being who he said he was terrified Bettie.

Absolutely terrified her.

CHAPTER 12
4th July 2022
Somewhere, Northern England
6:49 Hours Left

Graham was really unnerved about what happened to Mia Ford. But it actually made so much sense and whoever in MI5 had come up with this operation was extremely clever.

To Graham it was perfect to give the undercover or whoever these people were fake names and fake jobs, that would completely mask who these people really were, and more importantly how they were connected.

"Putting you on speaker phone Sean," Bettie said.

Graham lent on one of the luggage racks.

"Auntie," Sean said, "we managed to find things about all three of those people,"

"Start with the victim," Bettie said.

"Okay," Sean said, "turns out Leon Zinc was

born in France in the 1990s, went to school in the UK and is very much alive,"

Graham had been expecting it but it was still surprising to have it confirmed.

"Describe him Sean," Graham said, "and how you do know he's alive?"

"Harry searched social media, the Private Eyes databases and an MI5 one. Leon Zinc lives in Manchester and I spoke to him for about ten minutes. Pretending he had won some kind of competition,"

Graham smiled. "Good job. What about the other two?"

"The description?" Bettie asked.

Graham rolled his eyes. He had forgotten about that.

"Normally wears a red Bell Boy outfit for work, reasonably handsome and blue eyes," Sean said.

Graham heard Harry hit Sean gently, and that just made him smile. It was great to know that even after all of Harry's brain injuries and therapy, he was doing okay.

"That's him," Bettie said, "thank you. We'll call you back in a moment,"

Sean cut the line.

Graham turned around and started searching through the luggage.

"So these people look like their fake identities," Bettie said.

"Seems like it," Graham said. "Phone Sean back and ask him about Aubrey,"

"What? You don't believe she's a Politician,"

Graham shrugged. "You're seriously telling me a person that nice could work in politics,"

Bettie looked like she wanted to say something, but she dialled the Sat Phone again. Graham really wanted to ask her about that later.

"On speaker phone again Sean," Bettie said. "Need you to run a name for us. Aubrey Armstrong, Scottish Politician,"

"Harry do that for us babe," Sean said. "Thanks,"

Then Sean turned his attention back to the phone. "Alexander Bell is currently in London at some fundraising event. And William Jones is when it get interesting,"

Graham cocked his head and stopped searching through the luggage.

"Why?" Bettie asked.

"He was a Detective Inspector for the Met until two weeks ago. He was fired for criminal intent awaiting a full internal investigation. No one has seen him for two weeks,"

Graham just looked at Bettie. "So it's possible he's on the train,"

Graham heard someone take the phone off Sean.

"Affirmative," Carter said. "I vetted someone the train myself but everyone checked out,"

Graham shook his head. "That doesn't speak very highly for your skills. Mia, Leon and Alexander aren't who they say they are,"

Carter muttered something. Then Graham heard something in the background, and Sean pulled the phone away from Carter.

"Auntie, no one knows where Aubrey Armstrong is. There were tons of journalists camped outside her house, the First Minister's and every possible occasion where she could be. No one has seen her for two days,"

"What are the rumours?" Graham asked.

"Police aren't willing to comment after a body was found this morning in the River Ness. The Government aren't willing to comment either, but the media believe she's heading to London,"

Graham shook his head at that. How the hell did they know?

"Why?" Bettie asked.

"Because of a cock-up the Prime Minister made when a Scottish Politician asked him about Independence,"

Graham laughed. That was the most likely explanation and if there was one thing the Prime Minister was good at, it was making cock-up after cock-up, so Graham was hardly surprised.

"Thanks, Sean and Harry," Bettie said, "find out about that body for us,"

"Okay. Love you both," Sean said.

Graham really smiled as Sean cut the call. Then he returned to searching the luggage rack.

"You think the body's important?" Graham asked.

"A secretive train. A possible assassination plot. A body just happens to turn up nearby. It's at least worth a look," Bettie said.

Graham nodded. It made perfect sense, and he definitely wasn't wrong.

Graham finally found Leon's large black suitcase and pulled it off the top rack. He was surprised by how cold and heavy it was, it almost felt icy.

Bettie helped him place it on the floor and then Graham slowly opened it.

Graham was shocked to find guns, toxic syringes and a little black box device. There had to be enough guns to defeat a small army, this was ridiculous.

"Wow," Bettie said.

Wow was right. Graham was just too stunned to speak, there had to be a reason for all this. Graham just didn't know what the reason was.

Bettie picked up the black box device and smiled.

"I think this is a black market signal blocker," Bettie said as she checked the tiny label on the bottom, "and I think this makes us invisible to radar, internet and any other modern equipment,"

Graham shook his head. "That can't be right. What if there's another train on the tracks? We need to be seen. And we must have passed some stations along the way, their cameras must have seen us?"

Bettie shook her head. "I used to have the older model years ago, and these devices work. A little too well because they're illegal, but they work,"

"Why would a person pretending to be Leon

Zinc have an illegal signal blocker in his bag?" Graham asked.

"Whatever the answer," Bettie said, "is what will lead us to our killer,"

Graham could only nod to that.

They had another piece of the puzzle.

But neither one of them knew where it fitted.

CHAPTER 13
4th July 2022
Somewhere, Northern England
6 Hours Left

Bettie lent against the cold Driver's compartment door as she stared at Aubrey who was spinning around on the metal chair in the very centre of the compartment surrounded by tons of switches and buttons.

This entire thing had to be connected to her and everything seemed to be centred around this one woman, but Bettie couldn't think for the life of her why. Why the hell would the people on this train want her dead?

Bettie hated how cloak and dagger everything was about this train, she had actually considered breaking the Signal Blocker device she had found in Leon's luggage, but she wasn't sure that was the best move.

Right now everything seemed easy to control (or

relatively), if Bettie unblocked the signals then sooner or later the police would find out about the strange train, stop it and probably arrest everyone.

Meaning Bettie would be separated from Aubrey. Then she really was a sitting duck ready to die.

"You must have some idea who these people are," Bettie said.

Graham, who was standing behind Aubrey studying the scenery as it rushed past, nodded.

"I don't. All that happened was the First Minister asked me if I wanted to go to a meeting in London with the PM to discuss Independence," Aubrey said.

Graham laughed. "Don't you mean told,"

Aubrey smiled, and Bettie had to admit it was such a great smile. It wasn't like all the fake horrible smiles that politicians normally had, this was a real smile, because it was clear as day that Aubrey actually cared about everyone she met.

Bettie had never seen a politician like her before.

"Of course not," Aubrey said, "in Scottish Politics, I'm proud to say that everything is more civilised, kind and choice-based compared to UK politics. Sure the First Minister is my boss, but she isn't a tyrant,"

Bettie smiled. "I've watched your First Minister a few times, and I have to agree. It's certainly… there's certainly a lot less shouting and blame-calling in your politics,"

"And I'm sorry your politics is going through a rough patch at the moment," Aubrey said.

Bettie almost wanted to applaud her for that answer, sure she was a politician, but a normal one would have made some kind of remark about how much better Scottish politics was compared to UK ones, but surprisingly enough Aubrey seemed to respect it still.

Even though it far from respected her.

"That's why people want to kill you, isn't it?" Graham asked.

Aubrey shrugged. "Graham… I get hundreds of death threats a week. Some from the English, some from the Scots who are against Independence and some from lonely people who want someone to shout at,"

"Is one of those people here?" Bettie asked.

Aubrey shrugged. "You tell me. But this feels organised. First you had my allergic reaction, then you had the poisoned EpiPen then you had Mia's injection,"

Bettie nodded. She had a good point. Someone on this train had to be connected to all of it, and Bettie had to find out what linked them all, and why on earth give them all fake names?

"I think the names are the key," Bettie said.

Graham nodded and came to stand next to Bettie.

"Why pick those names in particular? Why pick fake IDs? Why not just makeup names?" Graham asked.

Bettie paced around the compartment. "Because

I can't believe Carter is involved. He says he personally vetted everyone on this train,"

"Could he be lying?" Aubrey asked.

Bettie clicked her fingers. "Why now? Why are you having the meeting now?"

Aubrey looked up at the ceiling for a moment. "I don't know. Um, I know the First Minister has had a lot of European support lately. I know at least five Heads of States that have said they would trade with an Independent Scotland,"

Bettie shook her head, she had heard the same news lately. It was amazing that a not-Head of State would cause such a positive international stir, but she felt like there was more to it.

"Your First Minister might have the international support, but what about in London?" Bettie asked.

Aubrey clicked her fingers. "The election. Next year there's a General Election and of course the Opposition to the Government has promised Scotland something. The current plans look… not promising but there are still plans,"

Bettie just looked at Graham. "Any insights?"

Graham smiled. "Scotland is not my country. No offence,"

"None taken," Aubrey said smiling.

"We are thinking the UK Government wants to look good and appealing to Scottish voters next year," Bettie said.

Aubrey laughed. "It's clever. The Government pretends to be interested in Independence to attract voters next year. Then all their Scottish MPs fill up Parliament and the Sottish Government is effectively kicked out of Parliament,"

"But if that's the plan, then why kill you?" Graham asked.

Aubrey frowned. "Maybe that isn't the plan thankfully,"

Bettie shook her head. "There has to be a reason why the meeting, this train and all these guests are happening now,"

"I agree," Graham and Aubrey said.

"And then there's Carter and... Arh! There are so many questions!" Bettie shouted.

Aubrey got up and hugged Bettie gently. "Carter,"

Bettie smiled and nodded. "How the hell did a trained MI5 operative fail to detect at least two people who weren't who they said they were,"

Aubrey nodded. "Exactly,"

Bettie had given the Sat Phone to Graham earlier because it was just plain uncomfortable, and now Graham was getting it out.

Bettie looked at Graham. "Call them,"

Graham dialled Sean.

The phone answered.

"Get back!" Sean shouted.

Bettie grabbed the phone.

"Help!" Harry shouted.

There was fighting.

Screaming.

A gunshot went off.

Then another.

Then another.

The line went silent.

"Sean!" Bettie shouted into the phone.

Graham and Aubrey sat in silence.

"Sean!" Bettie shouted.

Someone picked up the phone.

"Auntie," Sean said weakly.

"What happened!" Bettie shouted.

Someone started to breathe heavily into the phone and Bettie reckoned that Sean was hugging Harry, who was probably heavily breathing.

"Carter saw I had found something on the case. He tried to jump me. Harry attacked. They fought. I grabbed your gun and..."

Sean's voice went wobbly and Bettie hated to imagine what he was going through. She had never killed another person, but she knew Graham had so she passed the phone back over to him.

Graham started comforting him.

But Agent Carter was dead.

Their only lead was dead.

Bettie had to confront these guests.

She had to get to the truth.

No matter what.

CHAPTER 14
4th July 2022
Somewhere, Midlands England
6 Hours Left

"I'm going to take a gun to all their heads!" Bettie shouted.

Graham quickly hugged her and gently pressed her against the cold plastic walls of the Driver's compartment. He hated seeing her so annoyed, stressed out and rageful. He felt it too because no one dared to attack his family and got away with it, but Graham, Bettie and Aubrey needed to think clearly.

And as tempting as it was (Graham himself was extremely tempted) putting a gun to people's heads wouldn't solve anything.

Thankfully before Graham came in the Driver's Compartment to talk with Bettie and Aubrey, he had put the mini-camera that Bettie bought in the spyware shop in place, so all Graham needed to do was check his phone to see if anyone disturbed the body or

Leon's luggage filled with the guns, drugs and whatever some abominable things he dared to bring on the train.

Bettie kissed Graham and Graham looked into her sexy stunning eyes and took long deep calming breaths of the cold cherry-shortbread scented air. After a few moments Bettie copied and she calmed down.

Graham nodded at her and Bettie kissed him. She was thankfully calm now and Graham placed the Sat Phone in her hand and raised it to her ear.

Graham laughed when he saw a very small black button on the bottom of the Phone, he pressed it and then the Sat Phone was on speaker. He had no idea til now how the speaker function worked, thankfully Bettie had before now.

"Is Sean okay?" Graham asked.

"Yea," Harry said.

Graham was relieved he was sounding okay considering the brain injury, the stress of the attack and having to look after a traumatised Sean.

"What did you find?" Bettie asked.

Graham heard Harry kiss Sean on the head presumably, and then harry must have pulled a laptop or computer closer to him.

"Sean found picture six people woodland area maybe five year ago. Include Carter," Harry said.

Graham, Bettie and Aubrey just looked at each other. There were seven other people on the train including Aubrey, so why did this picture trigger

Agent Carter to attack?

"Describe the people," Bettie said.

"Look like peeps you described," Harry said.

Graham looked at Bettie. "This photo must prove these people on the train look like the people who's names they stole,"

"Yea," Harry said. "That what gather from Sean's searches those IDs,"

It was only now that Graham was realising how those injuries had affected his language, but Graham was still relieved that he was better now than he had been a few weeks ago.

"Harry," Bettie said, "search Carter's pockets for us please. Try to find a phone or something,"

Silence.

"What's wrong!" Bettie shouted.

Graham gently rubbed her arm.

Sean took the phone. "Someone must have heard the shots. Auntie! I can't go to prison! I was defending myself! Help me please!"

"Relax Sean," a man said on the phone line.

Everyone went silent.

Graham and Bettie looked at each other. There was something about the voice that sounded familiar to Graham, he just couldn't place it.

"Who is this?" Aubrey asked.

The man laughed. "Next time Bettie don't buy spyware from an actual spy,"

Graham and Bettie rolled their eyes. They both recognised the voice and it was great to hear their friend MI5 Agent Daniels' voice again. If anyone could help them, it would definitely be him.

But why had he been listening to them?

"Daniels," Graham said, "it is rude to listen to other people,"

"Is it so rude when that same person can call off the police?" Daniels asked.

Bettie smiled. "Why are you here?"

Daniels changed his accent from English to Scottish. "Because I thought wee mine help each other,"

Graham's mouth dropped a little. He had absolutely no clue that Daniels was Scottish, he had always acted so English.

Bettie waved her hands in the air. "Wait! Why do you Aubrey and Daniels have such perfect English accents?"

They both laughed.

Aubrey smiled. "I'll tell them Daniels. If the Scottish have learnt anything over the past four hundred years, it is the English only take you seriously if you're a white, straight English male. I'm white and straight but not an English man,"

Graham wasn't too sure on it, but judging by Bettie's frown she clearly knew differently. Then Graham realised how compared to Bettie's (a straight white woman) and Sean's (a gay white man) lives had been, he had lived a very easy life.

"The photo," Bettie said. "Was it taken in 2017 in the South Downs in Southern England?"

Graham clicked his fingers. He was pretty sure he knew where she was going with this, there had a been a very major incident at the time.

"Yea," Harry said.

Bettie looked at Graham. "Around July 2017, there was a rumour in the Private Eye world about a special military operation that was a training session in the South Downs,"

Graham nodded. "I remember it. We, the police, were called in to help secure a section of the woods near… Cobham. That tiny village in the middle of nowhere,"

"I think," Bettie said, "and the Private Eye consensus at the time was there was no military involvement. But security services were tracking someone,"

"How would Private eyes know about it?" Daniels asked.

Aubrey smiled. "You'll be surprised at the sources Private Eyes have access to,"

With that statement only, Graham wouldn't have been too surprised if Aubrey informed some Private Eyes friends of hers of certain details, but Graham was hardly in a proposition to judge.

"Definitely," Bettie said, "but you confirm it?"

Daniels huffed. "That's why I'm listening in. I think Carter was a rogue agent trying to stop and kill the idea of Scottish Independence,"

Graham shrugged. "Why the train then?"

Bettie gasped. "Was that photo the first and last

time Carter worked with a group of people?"

Everyone went silent.

"Yes," Daniels said.

Graham and Bettie just looked at each other.

"Are you telling me everyone on this train is a possible Government-trained assassin?" Graham asked.

Daniel was silent.

Sean coughed. "But what about William Jones? He's a-"

"A very highly trained and criminal Detective Inspector," Graham said, "that could have spent the past two weeks training for something,"

"Like this train," Aubrey said.

Daniels huffed. "I am saying you're on a train with assassin trained people,"

Graham felt his blood run cold.

"And they all want to kill me," Aubrey said.

"Yes," Daniels said.

Graham couldn't let that happen. Sure he might not be sold on the whole Independence thing, but he was not letting a woman die on his watch.

"And we still have 6 hours until we arrive in London," Bettie said. "We need to survive another six hours,"

Graham checked his phone and looked at the security feed from the mini-camera.

Graham hated what he saw.

He saw all the remaining passengers were picking up the guns and pistols from Leon's luggage and was loading them.

"Shit!" he said.

"Shit!" Bettie said.

Graham grabbed the Sat Phone. "Daniels. We need help now!"

"I can't," Daniels said. "I can't find you. All traceable signals are being blocked,"

Bettie whipped out the Signal Blocker device.

She threw it on the floor.

Graham stomped on it.

"Better?" Graham asked.

"What did you do?" Daniels asked.

Bettie rolled her eyes. "We smashed the Signal Blocker Leon was using,"

"Oh yea," Daniels said, "and I'm magically meant to suddenly pick out a secret train from the entire UK,"

Graham and Bettie nodded. He did have a point.

Graham heard something.

Footsteps were getting closer.

"Harry. Sean. Find us!" Graham shouted.

Bullets fired.

Exploding open the door.

Bullets ripped through the Sat Phone.

They were alone now.

Truly.

CHAPTER 15
4th July 2022
Somewhere, Midlands, England
5:55 Hours Left

Bettie grabbed Aubrey and threw herself against the horribly cold walls of the Driver's compartment. Bettie hated these killers. She was going to make sure everyone paid.

Bullets screamed through the air.

Shattering the glass window.

Train controls were shredded.

Then everything stopped.

It took Bettie a few moments to realise she hadn't gone deaf as she quickly recovered from the ear-splitting noise of the guns.

Bettie looked at Graham who was flat against the opposite wall, looking concerned, frightened and worried. He was probably more concerned about Bettie than himself.

"Give us the Scot," Alexander shouted.

Bettie was really starting to get annoyed at these idiots. It was ridiculous that Carter had hired all of his old friends again probably for "one last job" on behalf of the UK government, but now this was just dangerous.

And Bettie was under no delusions that if these people were willing to kill such a major political figure in Scotland. Then they would have no problem killing her and Graham.

"We need a plan," Aubrey said quietly.

"Give her to us!" someone shouted. Bettie didn't recognise the voice.

But that was the entire problem, she didn't know how to get out of this mess. They were outgunned, out-trained and Bettie had no clue how she would stop five highly trained government assassins without getting herself killed.

Bettie heard guns reload.

"You have until we count down to one," Alexander said.

"Three!" Noah shouted.

Bettie looked around. There was nothing she could use.

"Two!" William shouted.

Bettie was desperate. Graham didn't look like he had an idea.

"One!" Alexander shouted.

Bettie jumped into the firing line.

She watched as all the guests on the train lowered their weapons. But she had to admit the entire train smelt disgusting now with it stinking of burnt cherry shortbread from the firing of the guns.

"Give that woman to us now!" Alexander shouted.

Bettie just smiled at him. It was amazing how angry he was getting, and Bettie was starting to realise that he really hadn't counted on Bettie and Graham being on the train. Bettie wouldn't have been surprised if everyone had been just as shocked as each other about their so-called timely arrival to protect Aubrey.

William raised his gun. "I served as a cop for decades and never got my way. Now I serve others, hold a gun and do whatever I want. I like this way better,"

Bettie really understood why the Met police had let him go now, he clearly wasn't of sound mind and he seriously looked like a criminal as he smiled at her.

Bettie hated to imagine how quickly he would hesitate before he shot her given the chance. He probably wouldn't even hesitate for a millisecond.

"Time," Graham said quietly.

Bettie smiled. That was really the name of the game here, the train was still zooming towards London and they still had another six hours to go.

That was the time when Aubrey had to be dead by.

And with Sean, Harry and hopefully Agent Daniels trying to locate them, all Bettie needed to do was give them as much time as possible to find them.

But Bettie just knew that was easier said than done.

"Let's make a deal," Bettie said, smiling.

Everyone looked at Alexander and Bettie instantly realised he was the leader.

"What sort of deal?" he asked.

"Me and Graham give you Aubrey in exchange for three things," Bettie said, calmly.

She was surprised that she didn't hear Aubrey protest, moan or get concerned. That woman was damn well impressive, and Bettie wasn't sure if there was anything that scared her.

"Name your things," Alexander said.

Bettie bowed slightly. "You don't kill Aubrey for another five hours. You don't kill me and Graham. You make sure Aubrey's death is quick,"

Alexander sneered at Bettie like she was the most disgusting person on the entire planet.

William walked up to Bettie. Pointing the gun at her head.

A gun went off.

William's head exploded.

Covering Bettie's face in blood, bone shards and brain matter.

"Why five hours?" Alexander asked.

Bettie was still a little shocked by the death, and that Alexander was acting like it was nothing.

He wasn't normal!

"Miss English, why five hours?" Alexander asked.

Bettie took a deep breath of the blood-scented air that made the taste of metal form on her tongue.

"Because Mr Bell, I believe Aubrey deserves a few hours of peace before she dies. After all the UK Government is humane, or is that just a slogan?"

Alexander smiled. "Okay Miss English. You have yourself a deal. And please know, if anyone tries to kill Aubrey before your five hours is up, I will kill them first. And if you try to escape, I will kill you first,"

Bettie simply nodded.

She really hoped five hours would be enough for Harry and Sean to locate them.

If not. Bettie could have to create an escape plan.

And she only had five hours to create one.

And that terrified her.

Absolutely.

CHAPTER 16
4th July 2022
Somewhere, Near London, England
55 Minutes Left

Graham hadn't slept a single second for the past five hours. He had been too concerned, and as he sat next to Bettie and held her tight. He quickly realised that this stupid five hour limit was now up.

Aubrey was going to die.

"The flare," Graham said.

Bettie's eyes widened and Graham kept watch as Bettie slipped her hand under their train seats and went into the black bag from the spyware shop earlier and she retrieved the mini-flare.

Graham knew that the mini-flare couldn't be fired too close to them because it burning and the sparks would probably catch one of them alight. But somehow just knowing that they had a miniature (and extremely deadly) weapon gave him some kind of comfort.

It still bothered Graham though, because he was a cop. And cops do not kill people no matter how bad the situation gets, so Graham didn't want to have to use the flare gun.

But to protect this family, he would do whatever it took.

"Cop! Private Eye!" Doctor Noah shouted.

Graham slowly popped his head into the aisle to see Alexander preparing his pistol whilst a new lady and Noah pulled Aubrey up from her seat.

Graham didn't recognise the new lady in the slightest but there had always been a woman who had been hiding her face between a newspaper. So at least Graham finally got to see this mystery woman.

And Graham had to admit she was quite a looker with her smooth skin, amazing smile and the most stunning green eyes Graham had ever seen. (But Bettie's eyes were better, of course)

Alexander looked at Graham. "Both of you. Come here. Now!"

Graham looked at Bettie and he didn't see the mini-flare anymore, so he just hoped she had hidden it somewhere easy to get to.

Their lives might depend on it.

As Graham and Bettie walked along the train, the warm early morning sun caught their faces and skin, and somehow it felt like the last sunlight they would ever see.

Graham and Bettie stood next to each other when they reached the front of the train, and Graham frowned as he saw Aubrey had been pulled into the Driver's Compartment of the train and forced onto her knees.

But to Graham's surprise, and the darkest of last night must have hidden it, there was a large piece of flooring that had been ripped out. Revealing a metal lock of sorts that properly connected the Driver's Compartment to the rest of the train.

As crazy as it sounded to Graham, he actually wanted to use that connection somehow to save them.

"When I give the signal. Give me the flare," Graham said quietly.

Bettie subtly nodded.

Alexander walked straight up to Graham's face.

"How does it feel to know you've failed?" he asked.

Graham smiled. He hadn't failed until Aubrey was dead. And she was far from dead yet.

Aubrey hissed as Noah and the new lady wrapped their hands round her throat.

"Who's the new one?" Graham asked, hoping for some more time.

Alexander clicked his fingers and the new lady came out and gave Alexander a massive passionate kiss.

Then the woman punched Graham in the face.

He fell back.

Catching Bettie's arm.

Knocking the mini-flare out of her hand and it

hit the floor.

Alexander looked furious as he picked it up. Graham felt his stomach tighten as he forced himself up.

"What is this!" Alexander shouted.

Bettie smiled. "A gift,"

Graham didn't know what she meant.

The mini-flare activated. Bright fire shot out.

Graham pushed Bettie away.

Graham dived on Alexander.

Grabbing the flare.

Graham screamed.

He threw it at the metal joint.

The mini-flare smashed.

Blinding light shot out.

The train jerked.

Something snapped.

Something crashed.

Bettie gripped the chairs.

Graham flew forward.

Guns fired.

The train jerked again.

Graham dived on Alexander.

Whacking him.

The train slowed down.

Graham smashed Alexander's head into the ground.

Graham grabbed his gun.

Shooting him in the head.

But as Graham felt the cold metal barrel of an

automatic rifle against his head, he gulped and slowly raised his head as the train really slowed down.

When the train had basically crashed into the Driver's Compartment, it must have broken the controls and the connection between the train and the people controlling it in London, so the train was stopping.

Then the train gently rolled to a stop. Graham was grateful they hadn't been on a turn.

Graham felt the cold metal barrel press harder against his head as he stared into the cold eyes of the new lady, also known as Alexander's girlfriend.

Doctor Noah stood next to her and Graham was relieved to see he had a massive slice on his forehead.

But Noah fixed his gun on Bettie.

Graham stood on her toes for a moment, but he couldn't see if Aubrey was alive or not.

"I don't care what deal you made with Alexander," the new woman said. "On your knees,"

Graham looked at Bettie. He blew her a kiss. He loved her so much.

"On! Your! Knees!" she shouted.

They both nodded.

Graham moved closer to Bettie and as they were both on their knees, they held each other's hands just in case this was the last time.

"Don't worry," the woman said, "the Scot will join you very shortly,"

Two shots went off.

Noah's body dropped.

Someone boarded the train.

The new lady gasped. She raised her gun.

Two more shots fired.

The woman's blood splattered Graham's head as her body dropped.

Graham and Bettie slowly stood up and smiled as they saw Agent Daniels standing there smiling holding his pistol.

Graham and Bettie spun around.

They raced towards the Driver's Compartment.

They had to find Aubrey.

And against all the odds, Aubrey was just sitting there crawled up in the corner out of sight, her eyes were tightly closed, and the only injury she had were some minor cuts to her face.

Graham and Bettie hugged her.

They were alive.

They were all alive.

All the bad guys were dead.

And now Graham had to get Aubrey to her meeting. It was the least he could do.

CHAPTER 17
4th July 2022
London, England

As Graham stood outside a massive government building in the heart of London with its plain smooth bricks sending cold chills inside his back as he leant on it, he was extremely glad to finally be standing on solid ground.

Granted it was London ground, so it was smooth, unloved and a little tacky. But Graham was still so glad to be standing still and not on some evil train that wanted to kill him.

But to Graham's surprise he was actually starting to miss the smell of cherry shortbread that had been so abundant and wonderful in the train carriage. Now Graham could only smell the pollution, expensive perfume and aftershave that summed up London so perfectly for him.

It was still far better than being on the train though.

Graham stared at his beautiful sexy partner Bettie as she rubbed her baby bump lovingly as she leant next to him. Graham was definitely not going to be doing any more cases with Bettie until after the babies were born.

And Bettie had flat out agreed.

She had actually promised that she would stick to background checks for the next few months, and she would only go to Private Eye Con (or the British Private Eye Federation Convention as it was more officially known), and Graham couldn't believe a convention filled with know-it-all Private Eyes would be dangerous, so he was fine with it.

As Graham listened to the wonderful sounds of people talking, laughing and people playing music in the street, Graham was a bit surprised at how much he was enjoying the mundaneness of it all. He had heard the same terrible music so many times, but he loved it this time.

Because it really showed how back to normal the world was.

Especially, as it wasn't until MI5 had seized the secretive train carriage that Graham and Bettie had remembered that Mia Frost had still been breathing, and it turned out that Alexander had stuffed her into a cupboard.

So when Agent Daniels interrogated her, he had sneaked Graham, Bettie and Aubrey into the building so they could watch it.

Even now Graham was surprised at how

forthright she was being, she explained everything so clearly. Herself, Carter and all the other people on the train except Aubrey and William Jones had met years before on a training mission in the South Downs, where they were unofficially tracking down a terror suspect.

Over the course of the mission, they all got extremely close, they all shared their hatred towards the Scots and how out of order they were being about their demands for Independence, and even in the interrogation Mia still couldn't understand why the crazy Scots wanted to leave the Mighty United Kingdom.

Graham had actually bursted out laughing when she said that, Bettie and Aubrey were clearly surprised when he did that.

And when MI5 told Agent Carter about the top-secret meeting, they allowed him to conduct a "top-secret mission". Graham still felt sorry for Agent Daniels, he couldn't even begin to imagine what it was like to know that your organisation had turned a blind eye to this rogue op.

But there was one question Graham had waited until the end to hear. Aubrey had popped out multiple times because it was too painful for her to listen to all the crap Mia was coming out with, but Graham and Bettie had wanted to know why did Mia give Bettie the EpiPen that saved Aubrey's life.

And there was a very simple answer. One that really surprised all three of them.

It turned out Mia had wanted to turn on everyone else, kill Aubrey at a later date and return to UK Government a hero of the UK.

To Graham it was just so strange to hear an English person speak with such hate and coldness about the Scots and like they were an invading alien race.

There was no need for it.

But Graham had looked into the police databases and there were tons of English groups on social media that preached the same hate.

In a way it made Graham feel bad to be English, and now… now he really hoped the Scots did gain independence, because Aubrey was right. Every country should be able to decide its own future and not be ruled by a government a country didn't even vote for.

The sound of Aubrey laughing hard made Graham stand up and push away from the wall.

"What's up?" Bettie asked as Aubrey walked towards them.

Aubrey smiled. "It turned out I never had an appointment with the Prime Minister,"

Graham's eyes widened. That was impossible, Aubrey had showed him and Bettie the texts earlier.

"But you did," Graham said firmly.

Aubrey gave Graham such a warm smile. "Graham, you really are a great cop. But I was never meant to reach London. That meeting was just a reason to get me on that train and I was never meant to get off,"

Graham gasped. This was… disgusting. He couldn't even begin to imagine how long winded this assassin plot was and how far into the heart of government it had to reach.

Bettie folded her arms and smiled. "You know you would never have a meeting, didn't you?"

Aubrey nodded. "Of course not,"

"Then why come?" Graham asked.

"Because," Aubrey said, "no Scot hates the English, and no day there will be a government in Westminster that will want to hear our case for Independence and one day they will allow the Scottish people to choose their future,"

Graham could only nod. They really were the words of someone who loved her people and truly wanted the best for them, not through hate and violence, but through love, respect and peace.

And that was why Graham was surprised at how proud he felt for helping Aubrey today.

Graham stepped forward and extended his hand.

"Then I wish you the best of luck," Graham said, "and I truly wish you get your Independence,"

Aubrey pulled Graham and Bettie in for a hug.

"Thank you," Aubrey said, "you both really are amazing. If you ever need a favour, call me. I'm sure me and the First Minister can help,"

After a few moments, Aubrey pulled away from the hug and started to walk down the street.

Bettie's eyebrows rose. "How are you getting

back?"

"Catching a train," Aubrey said with a laugh.

Graham and Bettie just laughed. There really was nothing that could scare that amazing woman.

"But this time," Agent Daniels said behind them, "she will be under the ever-watchful eye of a Scot in English clothes,"

Graham nodded hard.

Then he took Bettie's hand and they both walked away. The case was over. The bad guys were gone.

And the good guys were safe.

And Graham just wanted to go home now.

CHAPTER 18
5th July 2022
Canterbury, England

After having two amazing wonderful chaotic days, having Sean drive her and Graham home, Bettie was so pleased to finally be back in her stunning office with its dark wooden walls, desk and her fabulous view out onto the cobblestone high street below.

Bettie seriously understood what Graham was talking about now when he mentioned how great it felt being on solid ground that wasn't moving. It felt amazing!

And Bettie hadn't realised until now how much she had missed her office, she loved Scotland, the travelling and the secret train journey. But she flat out loved her office. Especially as she had the window open slightly so she could listen to the amazing sounds of university students talking, joking and laughing with each other.

Even those simple sounds made Bettie feel so much more alive after the chaos of the past two days. And those simple sounds were how Bettie truly, truly knew that the world was about back to normal.

Bettie's favourite thing about her office, though, just had to be the wonderful bakery that was always cooking. Even now Bettie's office was filled with the most sensational smells of freshly baked bread that Bettie knew would melt into buttery deliciousness, creamy golden cakes and hints of pastries filled with succulent, crispy duck that Bettie was seriously looking forward to.

But despite all the chaos and danger and strangeness of the train case, Bettie had loved it. She loved helping people against the odds, protect and saving lives, because to her, that was what being a Private Eye was all about.

And she would never deny how much fun it was talking to Agent Daniels, because unlike all the MI5 stereotypes, he was just a good, kind and great man to be around.

Since it turned out William Jones had actually been fired because of some con Mia was running. She had created enough fake information about William's very real criminal activity that the leadership of the Met police had to fire him.

Then William was naturally annoyed so he was an easy target to manipulate and make him channel his aggression towards Aubrey.

Bettie still wasn't sure whether to be impressed

or not. It was so clever to be able to manipulate a person like that, but it was flat out wrong.

But Bettie's favourite bit of the case had to be Alexander's girlfriend who always hid herself behind a newspaper. Because she was the real leader and Alexander was nothing more than a puppet to make sure the more sexist elements of their rogue band of agents listened to her commands. Apparently she was one of the country's most prized agents before she started to become more and more of a far-right supporter, and that's when she started to take action against groups and people she didn't respect.

Bettie had utterly hated listening to all the war crimes, murders and even worse things she had committed against other people. And it was her that had bride Aubrey's private doctor (with the threat of torture) to reveal Aubrey's allergy.

Bettie was really glad she was dead.

As Bettie started to feel a little ill because of all the amazing smells of animal products and meat, she closed the window and slowly stroked her baby bump.

Bettie was rather pleased she had said she was going to give up fieldwork for a few months. It wasn't because she really wanted to, she loved being out in the world investigating crimes, she had to think about her twins now. That case had seriously bought that fact home, but at least Bettie got to go to Private Eye Con next month.

That was going to be great fun!

Someone knocked on the door.

Bettie slowly went over to the door and let in Graham who was really pleased to see her, and Bettie pleasantly surprised to see him. She had thought he would just go into work today, despite them giving him the rest of the week off.

Bettie cocked her head when she saw he was holding a police folder.

"Please tell me you haven't stolen another police file," Bettie said.

Graham jokingly hit her head. "Course not. I found out what happened to that body that was pulled out of the River Ness a few days ago. The body the Scottish Government and Police wouldn't comment on,"

Bettie nodded. That would be great to know.

"It was a middle-aged man who worked as a school teacher in Inverness," Graham said, "and the Police didn't want to comment on it because they were still investigating, and the government didn't want to comment because they respected what the police were doing. The government didn't want to interfere with the police just because it would make them look good,"

Bettie smiled. It might not have been case related, but she was still glad she knew. It had been bugging her for long enough, and at least it wasn't a missing puzzle piece of the train case like she feared.

"Bet," Graham asked slowly.

Bettie frowned slightly. She hated it when

Graham sounded so serious.

"What did you want to say to me yesterday when I said Aubrey couldn't be a politician because she was so nice?" Graham asked.

Bettie smiled and wrapped her arms around Graham.

"I don't know really. I just… I just want our children to grow up in a UK where the politics aren't so… hateful, disrespectful and rude. You only need to turn on the news to see politicians attacking and screaming at each other. And that's what I love about Scottish politics because they have everything we don't,"

Bettie wasn't sure how crazy or idealistic she sounded, but Graham just kissed her. Again. And again.

"Maybe one day those politics will return to Westminster but until that day," Graham said rubbing Bettie's baby bump, "we have to keep making the world a better place through our work,"

Bettie nodded. He was completely right.

"What cases you got?" Graham asked with a smile.

Pure excitement filled Bettie and Graham guided her over to her desk, and Bettie opened her laptop.

Whatever happened next was going to be amazing, fun and exciting because she was going to be working with the man she loved and helping the world become a better place.

Because that's all she ever wanted for herself, her

family and most importantly her unborn children.

GET YOUR FREE AND EXCLUSIVE SHORT STORY NOW! LEARN ABOUT NEMESIO'S PAST!

https://www.subscribepage.com/fireheart

Keep up to date with exclusive deals on Connor Whiteley's Books, as well as the latest news about new releases and so much more!

Sign up for the Grab a Book and Chill Monthly newsletter, and you'll get one **FREE** ebook just for signing up: Agents of The Emperor Collection.

Sign Up Now!

https://dl.bookfunnel.com/f4p5xkprbk

About the author:

Connor Whiteley is the author of over 60 books in the sci-fi fantasy, nonfiction psychology and books for writer's genre and he is a Human Branding Speaker and Consultant.

He is a passionate warhammer 40,000 reader, psychology student and author.

Who narrates his own audiobooks and he hosts The Psychology World Podcast.

All whilst studying Psychology at the University of Kent, England.

Also, he was a former Explorer Scout where he gave a speech to the Maltese President in August 2018 and he attended Prince Charles' 70th Birthday Party at Buckingham Palace in May 2018.

Plus, he is a self-confessed coffee lover!

Other books by Connor Whiteley:

Bettie English Private Eye Series
A Very Private Woman
The Russian Case
A Very Urgent Matter
A Case Most Personal
Trains, Scots and Private Eyes
The Federation Protects

The Fireheart Fantasy Series
Heart of Fire
Heart of Lies
Heart of Prophecy
Heart of Bones
Heart of Fate

City of Assassins (Urban Fantasy)
City of Death
City of Marytrs
City of Pleasure
City of Power

Agents of The Emperor
Return of The Ancient Ones
Vigilance
Angels of Fire
Kingmaker

The Garro Series- Fantasy/Sci-fi
GARRO: GALAXY'S END
GARRO: RISE OF THE ORDER
GARRO: END TIMES
GARRO: SHORT STORIES
GARRO: COLLECTION
GARRO: HERESY
GARRO: FAITHLESS
GARRO: DESTROYER OF WORLDS
GARRO: COLLECTIONS BOOK 4-6
GARRO: MISTRESS OF BLOOD
GARRO: BEACON OF HOPE
GARRO: END OF DAYS

Winter Series- Fantasy Trilogy Books
WINTER'S COMING
WINTER'S HUNT
WINTER'S REVENGE
WINTER'S DISSENSION

Miscellaneous:
RETURN
FREEDOM
SALVATION
Reflection of Mount Flame
The Masked One
The Great Deer

OTHER SHORT STORIES BY CONNOR WHITELEY

Mystery Short Stories:
Poison In The Candy Cane
Christmas Innocence
You Better Watch Out
Christmas Theft
Trouble In Christmas
Smell of The Lake
Problem In A Car
Theft, Past and Team
Embezzler In The Room
A Strange Way To Go
A Horrible Way To Go
Ann Awful Way To Go
An Old Way To Go
A Fishy Way To Go
A Pointy Way To Go
A High Way To Go
A Fiery Way To Go
A Glassy Way To Go
A Chocolatey Way To Go
Kendra Detective Mystery Collection Volume 1
Kendra Detective Mystery Collection Volume 2
Stealing A Chance At Freedom

Glassblowing and Death
Theft of Independence
Cookie Thief
Marble Thief
Book Thief
Art Thief
Mated At The Morgue
The Big Five Whoopee Moments
Stealing An Election
Mystery Short Story Collection Volume 1
Mystery Short Story Collection Volume 2

Science Fiction Short Stories:
The First Rememberer
Life of A Rememberer
System of Wonder
Lifesaver
Remarkable Way She Died
The Interrogation of Annabella Stormic
Blade of The Emperor
Arbiter's Truth
Computation of Battle
Old One's Wrath
Puppets and Masters
Ship of Plague
Interrogation
Edge of Failure

One Way Choice
Acceptable Losses
Balance of Power
Good Idea At The Time
Escape Plan
Escape In The Hesitation
Inspiration In Need
Singing Warriors
Knowledge is Power
Killer of Polluters
Climate of Death
The Family Mailing Affair
Defining Criminality
The Martian Affair
A Cheating Affair
The Little Café Affair
Mountain of Death
Prisoner's Fight
Claws of Death
Bitter Air
Honey Hunt
Blade On A Train

Fantasy Short Stories:
City of Snow
City of Light
City of Vengeance
Dragons, Goats and Kingdom
Smog The Pathetic Dragon
Don't Go In The Shed
The Tomato Saver
The Remarkable Way She Died
The Bloodied Rose
Asmodia's Wrath
Heart of A Killer
Emissary of Blood
Dragon Coins
Dragon Tea
Dragon Rider
Sacrifice of the Soul
Heart of The Flesheater
Heart of The Regent
Heart of The Standing
Feline of The Lost
Heart of The Story
City of Fire
Awaiting Death

CONNOR WHITELEY

All books in 'An Introductory Series':
BIOLOGICAL PSYCHOLOGY 3RD EDITION
COGNITIVE PSYCHOLOGY THIRD EDITION
SOCIAL PSYCHOLOGY- 3RD EDITION
ABNORMAL PSYCHOLOGY 3RD EDITION
PSYCHOLOGY OF RELATIONSHIPS- 3RD EDITION
DEVELOPMENTAL PSYCHOLOGY 3RD EDITION
HEALTH PSYCHOLOGY
RESEARCH IN PSYCHOLOGY
A GUIDE TO MENTAL HEALTH AND TREATMENT AROUND THE WORLD- A GLOBAL LOOK AT DEPRESSION
FORENSIC PSYCHOLOGY
THE FORENSIC PSYCHOLOGY OF THEFT, BURGLARY AND OTHER CRIMES AGAINST PROPERTY
CRIMINAL PROFILING: A FORENSIC PSYCHOLOGY GUIDE TO FBI PROFILING AND GEOGRAPHICAL AND STATISTICAL PROFILING.
CLINICAL PSYCHOLOGY
FORMULATION IN PSYCHOTHERAPY

PERSONALITY PSYCHOLOGY AND INDIVIDUAL DIFFERENCES
CLINICAL PSYCHOLOGY REFLECTIONS VOLUME 1
CLINICAL PSYCHOLOGY REFLECTIONS VOLUME 2
CULT PSYCHOLOGY
Police Psychology

A Psychology Student's Guide To University
How Does University Work?
A Student's Guide To University And Learning
University Mental Health and Mindset

Companion guides:
BIOLOGICAL PSYCHOLOGY 2ND EDITION WORKBOOK
COGNITIVE PSYCHOLOGY 2ND EDITION WORKBOOK
SOCIOCULTURAL PSYCHOLOGY 2ND EDITION WORKBOOK
ABNORMAL PSYCHOLOGY 2ND EDITION WORKBOOK
PSYCHOLOGY OF HUMAN RELATIONSHIPS 2ND EDITION WORKBOOK

HEALTH PSYCHOLOGY WORKBOOK
FORENSIC PSYCHOLOGY WORKBOOK

Audiobooks by Connor Whiteley:
BIOLOGICAL PSYCHOLOGY
COGNITIVE PSYCHOLOGY
SOCIOCULTURAL PSYCHOLOGY
ABNORMAL PSYCHOLOGY
PSYCHOLOGY OF HUMAN RELATIONSHIPS
HEALTH PSYCHOLOGY
DEVELOPMENTAL PSYCHOLOGY
RESEARCH IN PSYCHOLOGY
FORENSIC PSYCHOLOGY
GARRO: GALAXY'S END
GARRO: RISE OF THE ORDER
GARRO: SHORT STORIES
GARRO: END TIMES
GARRO: COLLECTION
GARRO: HERESY
GARRO: FAITHLESS
GARRO: DESTROYER OF WORLDS
GARRO: COLLECTION BOOKS 4-6
GARRO: COLLECTION BOOKS 1-6

Business books:
TIME MANAGEMENT: A GUIDE FOR STUDENTS AND WORKERS
LEADERSHIP: WHAT MAKES A GOOD LEADER? A GUIDE FOR STUDENTS AND WORKERS.
BUSINESS SKILLS: HOW TO SURVIVE THE BUSINESS WORLD? A GUIDE FOR STUDENTS, EMPLOYEES AND EMPLOYERS.
BUSINESS COLLECTION

GET YOUR FREE BOOK AT:
WWW.CONNORWHITELEY.NET

www.ingramcontent.com/pod-product-compliance
Lightning Source LLC
LaVergne TN
LVHW012113070526
838202LV00056B/5716